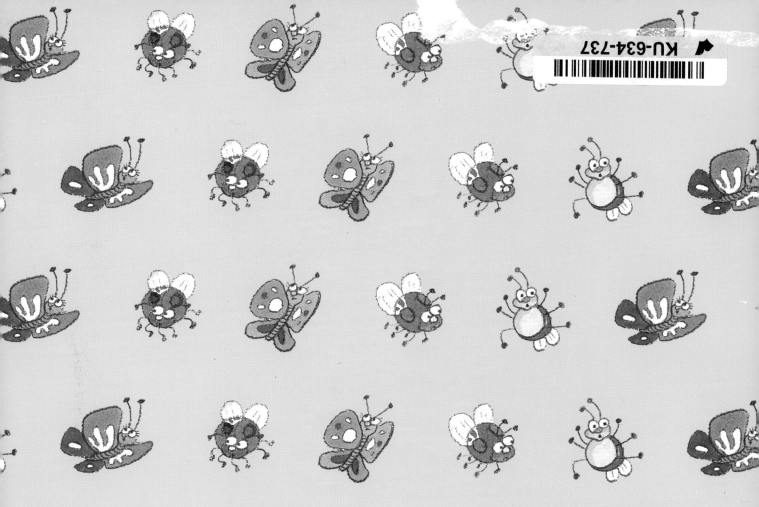

THE
BIG BAD
RUMOUR

And this one's for Oliver – J.M.

For my brother Ben – J.E.

First published in 2000

1 3 5 7 9 10 8 6 4 2

Text © Jonathan Meres 2000
Illustrations © Jacqueline East 2000

Jonathan Meres and Jacqueline East have asserted their right under the
Copyright, Designs and Patents Act, 1988, to be identified as the
author and illustrator of this work

First published in the United Kingdom in 2000 by
Hutchinson Children's Books
The Random House Group Limited
20 Vauxhall Bridge Road
London SW1V 2SA

Random House Australia (Pty) Limited
20 Alfred Street, Milsons Point, Sydney
New South Wales 2061, Australia

Random House New Zealand Limited
18 Poland Road, Glenfield
Auckland 10, New Zealand

Random House South Africa (Pty) Limited
Endulini, 5A Jubilee Road, Parktown 2193, South Africa

The Random House Group Limited Reg. No. 954009

www.randomhouse.co.uk

A CIP catalogue record for this book is available
from the British Library

ISBN 0 09 176954 X

Printed in Singapore

THE
BIG BAD
RUMOUR

JONATHAN MERES
& JACQUELINE EAST

HUTCHINSON

LONDON SYDNEY AUCKLAND JOHANNESBURG

'There's a big bad wolf coming
and he's hopping mad!'
cried the goggle-eyed goose,
all in a flap.

'*What's that?* There's a hopping mad wolf and he's bad and he's big?' cried the wittering weasel, whiskers twitching.

'*What's that?* There's a whopping bad wolf and
he's wearing a wig?' cried the jittery jay,
tail flicking.

'*What's that?* He's shopping mad and he's scaring a pig?' cried the harassed hedgehog, prickles prickling.

'*What's that?* There's no stopping him now he's so mean and scary?' cried the panicking polecat, mind racing.

'*What's that?* He's the size of a cow and incredibly hairy?' cried the muttering mole, nose dribbling.

NO, STOP!

'You've got it all wrong,' cried the observant owl, eyes blazing. 'Pay attention to *Goose*, don't listen to Mole!'

'*What's that?* He wrestled a moose and then swallowed him whole?' cried the frantic fox, brush bristling.

NO, NO!

'Quiet, everyone!' cried the goggle-eyed goose, in an even bigger flap. 'This is becoming *ridiculous!*'

'*Who is?* Who's coming to tickle us?' whispered the beetling beetle, shell shivering.

'Stop! Stop! Stop!' cried the goggle-eyed goose, in the biggest flap of all. 'Now – listen … very … carefully.'

THERE'S A BIG BAD WOLF COMING AND HE'S HOPPING MAD!

'Yikes! That'll be him now!
Quick, everyone, hide!'
Knock knock!
'Who's there?'

'A small sad wolf . . .'

'A small sad wolf?'

'Are you hopping mad?'

'No …'

'*You're not?* Phew!'

'I'm a small sad wolf and …

...I'VE BROUGHT
MY DAD!

TOLD YOU SO!

said the goggle-eyed goose.

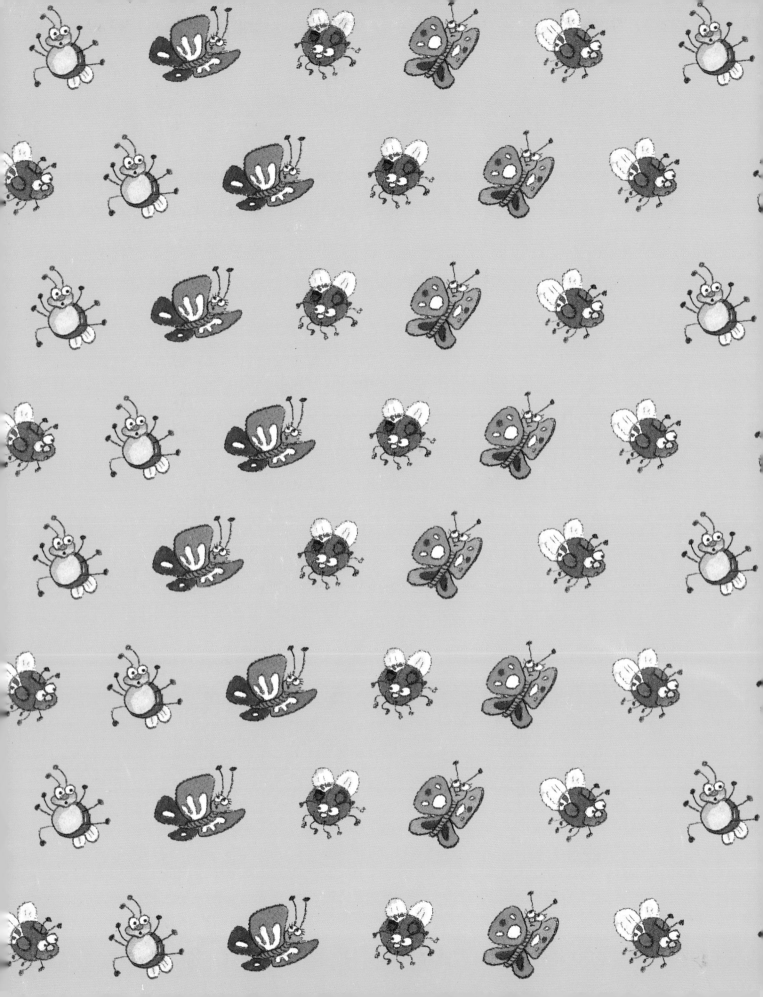